On a busy little street, in a busy little town,
there was a shop called 'Fox & Son Tailers'.

Rory's dad, Fox, was a tailer. His grandad was a tailer before that, and his great-grandad was a tailer before that.

THE O'BRIEN PRESS
DUBLIN

PADDY DONNELLY

Animals came from all over to have their tails made by him.

Rory helped his dad in the shop.

One of his jobs was to
measure the customers.

Sometimes, that wasn't so easy.

Fox & Son Tailers had tails for work,
tails for weddings,
tails for birthday parties,
and even tails for your first day at school.

But Rory was bored of tails.

He'd lost count of the number of times
he'd heard his dad say:

'Wedding Tails have to be 7 feet
3 ¾ inches long.'

or 'Formal Tails need
to be ⅞ of an inch
off the floor.'

'Why can't we do something
different for a change?'
Rory thought.

'What's all this?' asked Rory's dad.
'They're my ideas, Dad,' said Rory.
'Just imagine a big, long, feathery
tail with bright colours!
Or a spiky, slimy tail!
Or a fluffy, bouncy tail!'

But Rory's dad wasn't so sure.

'Tailering is a noble profession.

Our customers don't want silly things like this.

Now, stop playing around and fetch me

a box of safety pins!'

Rory did as he was told ...

or so his dad thought.

After everyone had gone to bed,

Rory sneaked into the workshop ...

and turned his 'silly things' into something fun.

'I just know the customers will **LOVE** these tails!' he thought.

The next day, a Very Important Peacock came into the shop.
'I'm looking for something rather special for a grand birthday party!' he exclaimed.
'Certainly, sir,' said Fox. 'We have a wide range of tails for you to look at.'

'How about this?'   'Or something   'These are very

'Oh, no!'   like this?'   popular right now.'

                    'No! No!'   **'NO! NO! NO!'**

'None of these will do,' said the Peacock. 'I need something **A-MAZ-ING**, something fabulous, something like … that!'

'Uh, oh,' thought Rory.

Fox gave Rory a look and said, 'Oh, that's just one of my son's wacky ideas. It's not for sale.'

'But this is just right!' said Peacock. 'I simply **MUST** have a tail made of these!'

'Now I'm in trouble,' thought Rory.

But Fox surprised him. 'I'm sorry I doubted you, son. When I was your age, I had wild and wonderful ideas too.

FOX TRIUMPHS AT TAIL SHOW

Now, if we're going to make this a-maz-ing tail in time, we'd better get started!'

And with that, Rory and his dad set out their tail-making tools.

They sketched and they dyed.

They glued and they tied.

They trimmed and they sewed.

And hoped it would hold.

For the final touch, Fox held the fabulous feathers as still as he could, while Rory painted on glowing tips and sparkling eyes.

'It's wonderful! It's marvellous! It's simply fabulous!'
said Peacock when he came to collect the tail.

'I'll be the talk of the town! And I'll make sure
EVERYONE knows where I got it!'

As the days went by, Rory dreamt up so many wild and wonderful tails.

There were long tails and short tails.

Furry tails and feathery tails.

Spiky tails and slimy tails.

Tails with beautiful colours.

Tails with stripes ...

tails with spots ...

and tails with both!

And the customers bought them **ALL**.

For weeks after, Fox & Son Tailers had a queue down the street. Everyone wanted one of Rory's terrific creations.

One night, Rory's dad gave him a present.
'Here, son. I've made something special
for us. It's my way to say thank you.'

'Oh wow!' said Rory, with a big smile.
'They're simply **FABULOUS**!'

Nowadays, Rory runs the shop.
Tails are available in all colours,
all shapes, all sizes ...

... and they've never been busier.

For my dad and my son, who helped with the tails – P.D.

Paddy Donnelly is an Irish author & illustrator living in Belgium, who has illustrated many children's books, including *Dodos Are Not Extinct*, *Here Be Dragons*, *Míp*, *The Last Seaweed Pie*, *Hom*, and *Wolves in Helicopters*. His work has achieved international acclaim and has been shortlisted for the World Illustration Awards and the KPMG Children's Books Ireland Awards. Paddy's first book as both author and illustrator, the award-winning *The Vanishing Lake*, is an intriguing and heart-warming story of a little girl, her grandad and a mysterious lake, and is also published by The O'Brien Press.

Paddy grew up on the beautiful north coast of Ireland, surrounded by mythical stories of giants, magical creatures and shape-shifting animals.
All of this prompted his love for nature, animals, the sea and storytelling.

First published 2023 by The O'Brien Press Ltd,
12 Terenure Road East, Rathgar, Dublin 6, D06 HD27, Ireland
Tel: +353 1 4923333; Fax: +353 1 4922777
E-mail: books@obrien.ie
Website: obrien.ie
Reprinted 2023.
First Published in hardback 2022.
The O'Brien Press is a member of Publishing Ireland.

Published in

DUBLIN
UNESCO
City of Literature

Growing up with
obrien.ie

ISBN: 978-1-78849-441-0

8 7 6 5 4 3 2
25 24 23

Printed and bound in Poland by Bialostockie Zaklady Graficzne S.A.
The paper in this book is produced using pulp from managed forests.

Praise for *Fox & Son Tailers*

'Celebrates the joy and importance of creativity, family love and relationships'
Books for Keeps

'A clever story with exuberant illustrations that are full of tiny details for young eyes to pore over.'
Sarah Webb, *Irish Independent*

'One of the most beautiful-looking books we've seen in a long time.'
RTÉ Guide

Fox & Son Tailers receives financial assistance from the Arts Council

the arts council
is chomhairle ealaíon | funding literature